A
Rookie
reader®

A Circle in the Sky

Written by Zachary Wilson
Illustrated by JoAnn Adinolfi

Children's Press®
A Division of Scholastic Inc.
New York • Toronto • London • Auckland • Sydney
Mexico City • New Delhi • Hong Kong
Danbury, Connecticut

Dear Parents/Educators,

Welcome to Rookie Ready to Learn. Each Rookie Reader in this series includes additional age-appropriate Let's Learn Together activity pages that help your young child to be better prepared when starting school. *A Circle in the Sky* offers opportunities for you and your child to talk about the important social/emotional skills of **natural curiosity and imagination**.

Here are early-learning skills you and your child will encounter in the *A Circle in the Sky* Let's Learn Together pages:

• Shapes
• Rhyming
• Story order: 1, 2, 3

We hope you enjoy sharing this delightful, enhanced reading experience with your early learner.

Library of Congress Cataloging-in-Publication Data

Wilson, Zachary, 1975-
  A circle in the sky / written by Zachary Wilson ; illustrated by JoAnn Adinolfi.
    p. cm. -- (Rookie ready to learn)
  Summary: A child puts together various simple shapes to build a rocket that will fly to the moon. Includes suggested learning activities.

  ISBN 978-0-531-26446-1 — ISBN 978-0-531-26746-2 (pbk.)

  [1. Shape--Fiction. 2. Rockets (Aeronautics)--Fiction. 3. Stories in rhyme.]
  I. Adinolfi, JoAnn, ill. II. Title. III. Series.
  PZ8.3.W6998Cir 2011
  [E]--dc22   2010049893

1 2 3 4 5 6 7 8 9 10 R 18 17 16 15 14 13 12 11

I see a circle in the sky,
white and shining bright.

I have some shapes and want to build . . .

a rocket to fly to
the moon tonight.

I will use a rectangle door . . .

so I can go inside.

I will use a circle window . . .

so I can see outside.

I will use a triangle top . . .

to point me to the sky.

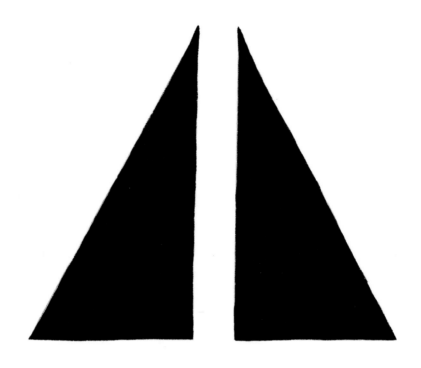

I will use triangle wings . . .

so my rocket ship can fly.

On the bottom I will use a square . . .

to push my rocket into the air.

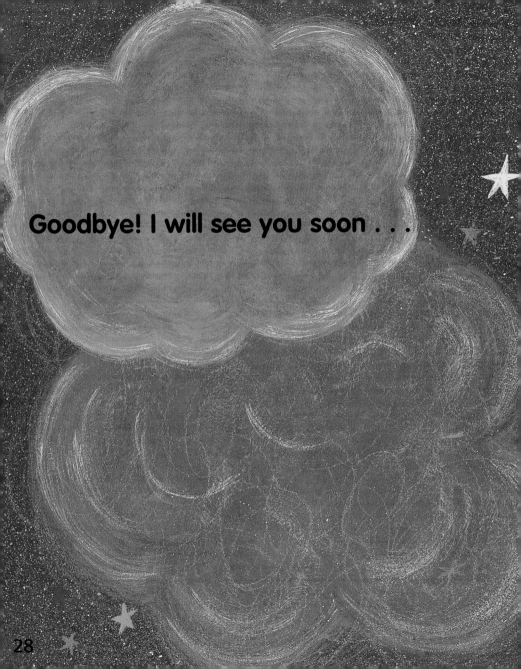

Goodbye! I will see you soon . . .

when I get back from my trip to the moon.

Congratulations!

You just finished reading *A Circle in the Sky* and found out what amazing things you can do when you use your imagination and put shapes together!

About the Author
Zach Wilson is an art teacher in New Jersey. He enjoys working with children of all ages and looks forward to writing more books.

About the Illustrator
JoAnn Adinolfi has illustrated many books for children. She was born and raised in Staten Island, New York, and now lives in Portsmouth, New Hampshire, with her husband and two children.

Rookie READY TO LEARN

ACTIVITY BOOK

A Circle in the Sky

Let's learn together!

Shapes Are Everywhere

(Chant this poem while drawing shapes in the air with your fingers.)

Circle, circle,
draw one in the sky.
Circle, circle,
round as a pie.

Square, square,
one, two, three, four.
Square, square,
like ceiling, walls,
and floor.

Rectangle, rectangle,
here's one more.
Rectangle can be a
shelf or a door.

PARENT TIP: After saying this rhyme, invite your child to find everyday objects with you that show the different shapes. For instance, a plate is a circle, a picture frame can be a square or rectangle, and a stop sign is an octagon.

First, Next, Last

The little girl worked hard to build her rocket ship. Take a close look at each picture. What is happening? Point to the picture that tells what happened **first**. What happened **next**? Which comes **last**?

PARENT TIP: Ask questions to help your child recall what is happening in each picture. What will the girl do with the shapes? Where is the rocket ship going? Talking with your child about what is in each picture and which events happened first, next, and last is a way to help her develop reading comprehension skills.

Shape Hunt

Say the name of each shape as you trace it with your finger. Then find each shape on the rocket. Once you find all the shapes on the rocket, say "3, 2, 1, blast off!"

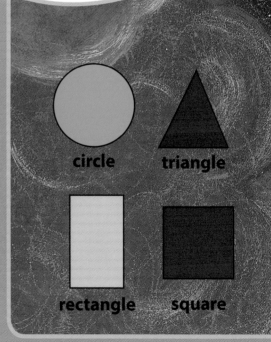

circle   triangle

rectangle   square

PARENT TIP: Another way to help your child become familiar with different shapes is to cut some from construction paper. Then invite your child to make his own rocket with the shapes. Glue it to a larger piece of paper. Or simply cut out shapes and invite your child to make anything he wants.

Would you like to go to the moon like this little girl imagined?

Look at the picture. What do you think it would feel like to walk on the moon? What would you do there?

PARENT TIP: Look at the moon with your child on different nights. Point out the changing shape: When the moon is full, it is a circle. When it wanes, it is a crescent. Encourage your child to draw the moon in its different stages on a piece of paper or a calendar. Projects like this can encourage early scientific thinking and observation skills.

Star Light, Moon Bright

Create your own night sky with this fun project.

YOU WILL NEED: White paper   Glue stick

Black paper ⬛ **Star stickers (optional)**

1
Cut out a circle and star shapes from the white paper.

2
Glue the moon and stars on the black paper. If you have star stickers, stick them on the paper, too.

3
Look at your picture and say: "Star light, moon bright, in the dark sky at night. A circle's in the sky tonight. Every night can have some light."

God bless all those that I love;
God bless all those that love me;
God bless all those that love those
that I love,
And all those that love those
that love me.

A Circle in the Sky Word List (52 Words)

a	goodbye	rocket	triangle
air	have	see	trip
and	I	shapes	use
back	in	shining	want
bottom	inside	ship	when
bright	into	sky	white
build	me	so	will
can	moon	some	window
circle	my	soon	wings
door	on	square	you
fly	outside	the	
from	point	to	
get	push	tonight	
go	rectangle	top	

PARENT TIP: Point to the words *my*, *rocket*, *ship*, and *trip*. Play an imagination game with your child. Say, "I am going on a rocket ship, and on my trip I will take…" Then take turns naming what you might take on your trip to the moon. If your child is familiar with beginning letter sounds, you can take turns naming things that begin with the letters *a*, *b*, *c*, and so on, until you get through all the letters in the alphabet.

To

- -

From

- -

- -

2021 First Printing This Edition

My Guardian Angel

Written and compiled by Sophie Piper.
Illustrations copyright © 2013 Sanja Rescek.
Original edition published in English under the title My Guardian Angel by Lion Hudson IP Ltd,
Oxford, England. This edition copyright © 2013 Lion Hudson IP Ltd.

ISBN 978-1-64060-758-3

The Paraclete Press name and logo (dove on cross) are trademarks of Paraclete Press.

The prayer on the back cover is by Isaac Watts (1674–1748). All unattributed prayers are by
Sophie Piper, copyright © Lion Hudson. Prayers by Lois Rock are copyright © Lion Hudson.
Bible extracts are taken or adapted from the Good News Bible published by the Bible Societies and
HarperCollins Publishers, © American Bible Society 1994, used with permission.

Library of Congress Control Number: 2021948543

10 9 8 7 6 5 4 3 2 1

Published by Paraclete Press
Brewster, Massachusetts
www.paracletepress.com

Manufactured by Dongguan P&C Technology Printing Co., Ltd.
Printed November 2021, in Dongguan, Guangdong, China.
This product conforms to all applicable CPSIA standards.
Batch 202111001P&C

Sophie Piper *Illustrated by* Sanja Rescek

My
Guardian
Angel

PARACLETE PRESS
Brewster, Massachusetts

Contents

Guardian angel
through the day
guide my steps
along the way.

Guardian angel
through the night
bring me safe
to morning light.

If I were an angel
then I would wear white
and only do things
that I knew to be right.

I'd put on a halo
of glittering gold
and I would be gentle
and I would be bold.

I'd flit through the world
on my soft feathered wings;
I'd speak words of kindness
and joyfully sing.

Praise the Lord with trumpets –
all praise to him belongs;
praise him with your music,
your dancing and your songs!

13

I don't feel afraid
to look up to the sky
and its miles and miles of blue;
for in the clear air
and the wide everywhere
is the love that surrounds me and you.

May my hands be helping hands
For all that must be done
That fetch and carry, lift and hold
And make the hard jobs fun.

May my hands be clever hands
In all I make and do
With sand and dough and clay and things
With paper, paint and glue.

May my hands be gentle hands
And may I never dare
To poke and prod and hurt and harm
But touch with love and care.

Love is giving, not taking,
mending, not breaking,
trusting, believing,
never deceiving,
patiently bearing
and faithfully sharing
each joy, every sorrow,
today and tomorrow.

For blessings here
and those in store
we give thanks now
and evermore.

Thank you for the little things
we notice every day
that shine on earth
with heaven's gold
and cheer us on our way.

The little bugs that scurry,
The little beasts that creep
Among the grasses and the weeds
And where the leaves are deep:
All of them were made by God
As part of God's design.
Remember that the world is theirs,
Not only yours and mine.

I am little
I am lowly
God is great and
God is holy;

yet was born
a child like me
here on earth
for all to see;

heaven's angels
bright and holy
watched his cradle:
little, lowly.

For his sake
eternally
angels will
watch over me.

When all the world is scary
and makes me feel so small
an angel takes my hand and says
that God is Lord of all.

The angel says, "God loves you,
there's nothing you need fear.
So come: let's walk on bravely
for I am always here."

Making amends
is an uphill road
and stony is the way.
At the top of the hill
you will find the gate
to a bright new shining day.

I give you the end of a golden string,
Only wind it into a ball,
It will lead you in at Heaven's gate
Built in Jerusalem's wall.

Easter sunrise angels
tell of God's great love:
Jesus is alive
and leads the way
to heaven above.

Angels, help me follow
though the way be long.
Guard me now and always.
Cheer me with your song.

May my life shine
like a star in the night,
filling my world
with goodness and light.

I close my eyes
and try to pray
but daydreams steal
my prayers away.
May some good angel
come close by
and take my prayers
to God on high.

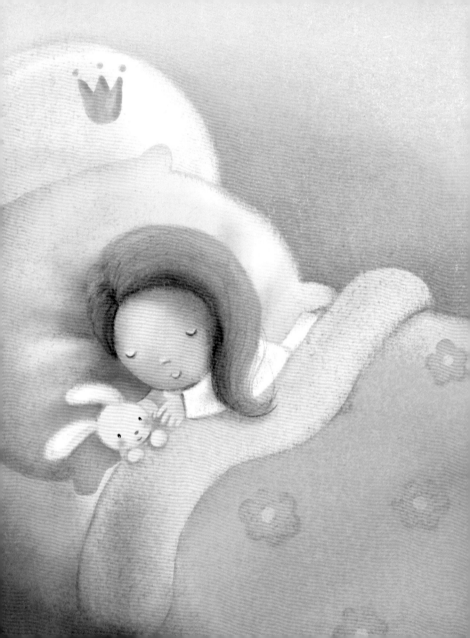

Lord, keep us safe this night,
Secure from all our fears;
May angels guard us while we sleep,
Till morning light appears.

Cradle me, kind angels,
In a coracle of darkness
Float me on the starry silver sea
Let me drift away
Through the waves of cloud and grey
To the land where
The morning waits for me.

Holy angel,
dim the light,
calm all worry,
still the night.
Keep me safely
in your sight.
Bring the new day
clear and bright.